Steamduck

Learns to FLY!

Written by:

Emilie P. Bush

Illustrated by:

Dedications:

To all the teachers, gurus and guides who have shaped me along my path, especially my father, who said, "You are what you think you are." ~ E.P.B.

To Darlene Dufour, for kind words and good advice. ~ W.K.P.

Steamduck Learns To FLY!

Written by: Emilie P. Bush

Illustrated by: William Kevin Petty

Layout design and color by: Theresa MeiHwa Curtis

STORIES

ISBN-10: 0984902813
ISBN-13: 978-0-9849028-1-1

Be sure to read other books from Coal City Stories, including Her Majesty's Explorer: a Steampunk bedtime story.

What all the world knew of a mechanical duck
was he paddled through streams and in lakes.
And the waddling tail of a mechanical duck
was for splashing and trailing through wakes.
His bill could blow bubbles, and sand was no trouble
as still waters were cut by his keel.
His cogs kept him swimming
on the surface
he's skimming,
the duck thought
for sure
he was real.

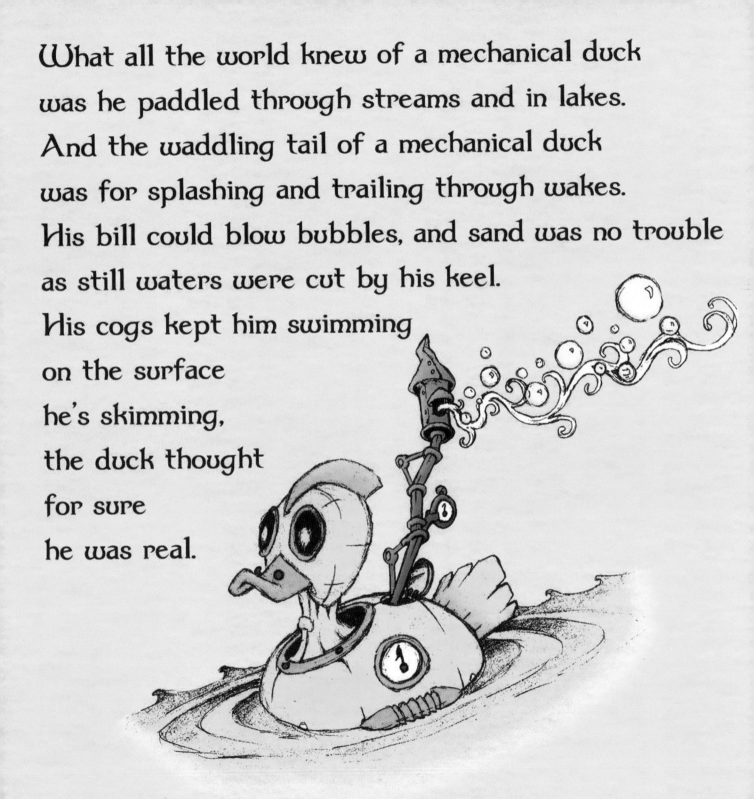

The spirit was plucky in our mechanical ducky,
'til a bright sunny day just last spring.
He swam round the bend
and our little friend
sighted a marvelous thing.

High in the sky, it caught Ducky's eye,
a goose floated and bobbed in the air.
It circled behind him then landed beside him
and Ducky did nothing but stare.

"Honk!" said the goose as he shook his wings loose, and then repeated twice more. "Honk Honk?" he inquired with a voice that was tired,

"Hey, why not take off and soar?"

With a sad "Quack!" for the choice he did lack. Duck said to Goose "I don't fly."

"That's quite a shame.
Go home and explain
to the inventor that you want to try.
Sort through this bother
with that clever old otter,
and soon, you and I will skim clouds."

To Ducky's dismay
the goose flapped away
without answering
Duck's where,
when or hows.

Steamduck returned
to the kindly old tinker
to put forth his request to take flight
He found in the shed the kindly old tinker,
squinting as the day lost its light.

"I want to fly," Ducky started to cry, and he wept with his heart in his throat.

"Real birds take wing, and see, here's the thing, I'm made not to soar – just to float."

"You float – it's true.
But, will any flight do?"
the old otter asked with a wink.

"I'll teach you tonight about all kinds of flight

and then we will sit down to think,
How to ascend... We'll do it friend,
for a real duck

fulfills both his callings:

To swim in the damp,
and there you're a champ,
and soon take the air
without falling."

Out of a nook Otter grabbed a thick book
that said "World of Flight" on the spine.
There on page one, with the lesson begun,
the terms were all clearly defined.
"Here's where we start, with the history part,
and two brothers - Montgolfier*.
They watched the smoke, in a genius stroke,
filled a bag and it floated away.

Air that is hot trumps air that is not.
That's how a hot air balloon rises.
The key here is LIFT,
it's a marvelous gift,
and now for more flight surprises...

1783

*[mont GAWL fee ay]

Otter drew pictures as Steamduck took notes
and the pair studied, thought and deduced.
Otter recited as Steamduck delighted
in the brainstorm the tinker produced.
From rocket to glider the choices got wider,
and Ducky's weak head got too full.
Decisions, revisions, about flying precision,
the thoughts got all itchy -- like wool.
"Sleep on it, Duck, and when we wake up,
we'll try each idea, by and by."
Otter wished good night, turned out the light,
and Steamduck sat waiting to fly.

When the dawn broke, the otter awoke, saying
"Steamduck! Today you take flight.
The sky is clear and you, my dear,
will be up in the air by tonight!"
Grabbing their gear, and a cold ginger beer,
they climbed atop Coal City Hill,
The ducky waddled and the otter tottled and they
felt the morning's chill.

The otter strapped to Steamduck's
back a complex web of bands.
With coughs and pops so turned
the props, and
Otter clapped
his hands.

The propeller pushed and Steamduck smooshed
his bill into the dirt.
In their thrift -
they forgot the LIFT!
At least Ducky wasn't hurt.

The otter thought through, how to raise
Ducky up, he thought with his
bubbly drink.
The otter found answers-
the fizz in his cup -
and knew what to do in a blink.
"The props, we've found, will push you round,
but we need a great big balloon.
One lighter than air, to get you up there,"
and Otter then penned a cartoon.
With one tiny sketch, he knew what to
fetch, and Ducky rolled to the old
tinker's shop. Returning with sheets,
and a couple of sweets, they cut and
they taped and they chopped.

At half past one they were finally done,
and they filled their newly made bag.
Fat with hot air, in the afternoon glare,
the pair encountered a snag.

They left open the latch.
Duck's NOT attached!

Softly, the balloon flew away.
Ducky, he cried. The old otter sighed
over a very good plan gone astray.
"Try, try again, my old metal
friend, but I think that I'm
fresh out of sheets,"
The old otter said
while scratching
his head, "We
cannot give
in to defeat."

Duck said
feeling blue,
"Oh, what will we do?
Balloons and props?
Tried and failed. Three-quarters gone,
our times near done, NO TIME!"
sweet Ducky wailed.

From out of the sun a great noise rocked the sky, as a copter flew right overhead.

Under the sun, the pair thought to try, and all around, the right tools were spread.

First they inspected through parts disconnected
until they found just the right things:
flaps and a motor, two skids and a rotor, and scoops
of cogs, sprockets and rings.

Built by Otter, a fine gyrocopter sat ready in time
for tea. The tinker snacked while Ducky quacked,
"I love what you built for me."

The otter smiled then turned a dial
in the middle of Ducky's chest.
Steamduck wheezed, couched and sneezed
and shook from tail to crest.

With the twang
of springs,
he sprouted
wings,
and, oh, how
they shined
in the light.
He moved
them round,
flapped up
and down,
and marveled
with total delight.

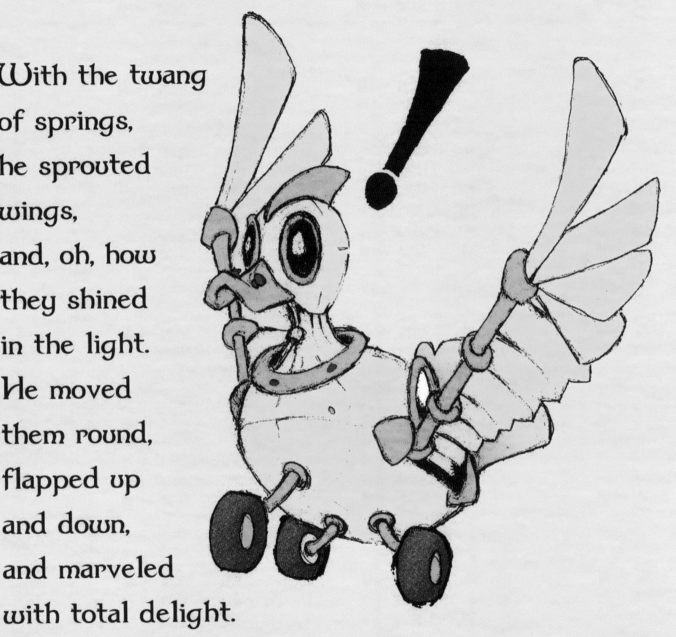

"No, my friend, in the end,
I think that you will find
I intervened with this machine
so I won't be left behind.

You were wrong, all along,
you were not a flightless thing.
As intended you were invented
with internal folded wings."

"You had to find them on your own,
and then you'd know you're right.
Aviation! Imagination!
You, too, were built for flight.
With what you've learned, you now have earned
the knowledge to take the sky.
With a running start and a clockwork heart,
we'll give it one last try."

Ducky flapped and wingtips tapped
the dirt as down he ran.
With splendid joy this wind-up toy
exclaimed as flight began,

"Watch me, Otter, watch me fly!
I swoop! I glide! I soar!
No more a boat just made to float,
I'm really something more!"

Otter hovered as duck discovered
ALL the gifts of flight.
They dipped and rolled as the day grew old
and the evening lost its light.
Back on the ground, Duck's wings turned round
and folded out of view.
From bill to tail, from flight to sail
no ducky was more true.

About the Author:
Journalist and writer Emilie P. Bush has written two children's book and two novels. Her Majesty's Explorer was a best seller. Her first novel, Chenda and the Airship Brofman, was a "ripping good yarn!" and the tale was a 2010 Semi-finalist for the Amazon Breakthrough Novel Award. The Gospel According to Verdu picks up the epic tale where Chenda left off - high in the skies.
Emilie P. Bush lives, laughs and writes in Atlanta.

ALLIED AETHERNAUTICS, LTD

About the Illustrator:
William Kevin Petty is the founder of Allied Aethernautics, LTD., a Steampunk illustration company and specializes in exceptionally detailed pencil sketches and and acrylic paintings. His work has appeared in Steampunk Magazine and across the web. See more of his work at www.allied-aethernautics.com. Mr. Petty lives and draws in central Louisiana.

About the Layout Designer:
Theresa MeiHwa Curtis's creative talents can be found in many art fields, working in layout design, photo editing, costuming and web creation. A passionate children's story collector, she has done layout and color for two picture books. Mrs. Curtis's family and her friends in the Atlanta Steampunk Community enjoy her exquisite costume design and tailoring. Theresa MeiHwa Curtis lives in the Atlanta area with her creative and loving husband, Mark.

Made in the USA
Lexington, KY
10 December 2012